The hero Beowulf

Retold and adapted by Eric A. Kimmel
from the epic poem *Beowulf*

Pictures by Leonard Everett Fisher

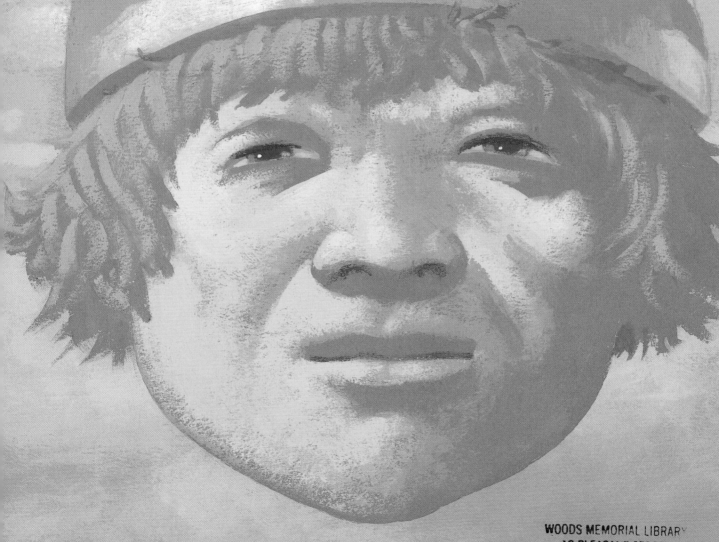

Farrar, Straus and Giroux

New York

Beowulf, son of Ecgtheow, had been a hero since childhood. When barely ten years old, he borrowed his father's sword to attack a nest of savage trolls that preyed on travelers passing through the mountains. He struck them left and right. After his blade broke, he ripped up an oak tree by its roots and battered the trolls until all lay dead.

Beowulf carried the heads of the trolls back to his father, along with their treasure and a magical troll-sword to replace the one he had broken.

That was Beowulf's first great deed. Others followed. As a young man on his first sea voyage, he sailed into stormy seas caused by the writhing of five sea serpents. They raised their heads above the rolling waves, each one higher than the ship's mast.

The serpents seized five sailors, swallowing them whole. Beowulf's companions dropped their oars in terror. They cowered behind their rowing benches, crying to the gods to save them.

Beowulf did not wait for the gods to answer. He slipped a dagger between his teeth. Leaping overboard, he swam to the nearest monster. He thrust his dagger between its scales until the creature floated away dead, its blood staining the waves.

The other sea serpents dived to the bottom of the ocean. Beowulf took a mighty breath and followed them. He hacked and thrust until he killed each one. He slashed open the corpses and freed his companions. All returned alive to the ship.

From Ireland in the west to Sarkland in the east, skalds and bards sang of the mighty deeds of Beowulf. However, his greatest adventure was yet to come.

Beowulf was attending his lord, King Hygelac, when he heard a horrifying tale from across the sea. A savage monster named Grendel was ravaging the land of the Spear-Danes. Hrothgar, their king, could do nothing to stop him.

The creature lurked in swamps and fens. He came out at night to attack Heorot, Hrothgar's beautiful hall. Grendel would seize Hrothgar's bravest fighters and devour them. Not a single man of Hrothgar's mighty host dared challenge the fiend, for the warrior who tried would be carried off into the shadows and never seen again.

"I will defend King Hrothgar," Beowulf said. "I will drive this foul creature Grendel from Heorot Hall or die in the attempt."

Beowulf pulled on his shirt of chain mail. He placed his helmet on his head and buckled his sword around his waist. Together with fourteen of his bravest companions, he set sail.

The ship flew across the ocean like a seabird. The wind caressed her back. Seafoam covered her bow.

Soon the high cliffs of the Danish land came into view. Beowulf and his companions pulled their ship onto the beach. They armed themselves for battle. Together they marched off to meet Hrothgar.

Beowulf arrived at Heorot Hall. "This is Beowulf," King Hrothgar told Wealhtheow, his queen. "I knew him when he was a boy. His father, Ecgtheow, was a mighty warrior. Now I see that his son exceeds him."

Wealhtheow welcomed Beowulf as an honored guest. "We are safe here while the sun shines," she said. "But as night comes, we must leave. When shadows fall, this place belongs to the monster Grendel."

"He gives us no peace," Hrothgar added. "He has consumed the bravest of my fighting men, gnawed the bones of my noblest companions."

"Grendel will pay for what he has done," Beowulf vowed to Hrothgar and Wealhtheow. "I promise that your friends will be avenged. My men and I will sleep tonight in Heorot Hall. When Grendel comes, I will fight him."

"Is there anything you require?" the king asked. "I have chests filled with bright swords and armor, sharp-edged spears and shining helmets. They are open to you. Take what you need."

Beowulf unbuckled his sword. He pulled off his chain-mail shirt and his helmet, placing them at the king's feet. "Since Grendel uses neither sword nor shield, neither shall I. Let no one say that I had an unfair advantage over him."

Beowulf opened the hall's oak door. Facing the fens and salt marshes, he cried out in a voice that could be heard all the way to the sea. "I, Beowulf, son of Ecgtheow, challenge Grendel to unarmed combat. It will be a fight to the death—strength against strength, cunning against cunning. If I win, Heorot Hall will be free at last. If Grendel wins, he may feast on my corpse in his foul lair below the marshes."

"Are you not afraid?" King Hrothgar asked.

Beowulf shrugged as he closed the door. "Why should I fear? If I am fated to win, then Grendel cannot defeat me. If I am fated to lose, then it has been my destiny since the day I was born. Neither I nor anyone alive can change it."

"This is a true hero," Hrothgar said to his queen.

"May the gods watch over him. May we find him alive and well in the morning," Wealhtheow answered.

The evening shadows came on. Hrothgar, Wealhtheow, and all their company withdrew to safety, leaving Beowulf and his companions alone in the hall. They lay down on the sleeping benches. Dark thoughts filled Beowulf's mind as his friends closed their eyes in slumber. He wondered if they would ever see their homes and families again.

Beowulf listened. He heard the monster rising from the marsh. He heard Grendel's footsteps approaching Heorot Hall.

The monster tore the iron-bound door from its hinges and burst inside. Green slime dripped from the scales covering his body. His two arms reached below his knees. Each hand ended in three claws, curved blades that could rip the life out of any man or beast that crossed the creature's path. He seized the nearest man.

Beowulf watched the horror through half-closed eyes. His friends grabbed their weapons. Only Beowulf remained still, waiting for Grendel to come to him.

Grendel stalked toward the man he believed to be sleeping. "An easy meal!" the creature rasped. He raised his arm, striking down with his dreaded claws.

Beowulf clutched the monster's wrist. "If you want this dinner, you'll have to fight for it."

Grendel writhed and twisted, trying to free himself. "Who are you? You cannot be a mortal. Never have I encountered such strength in a human being. Tell me your name!"

"I am Beowulf, son of Ecgtheow," Beowulf answered, tightening his grip.

"Release my arm!"

"I will let go when you are dead."

Beowulf's companions joined the fight. They struck at Grendel with sword and ax, spear and dagger. But they made no wound, not even a scratch, for the scales covering Grendel's body were enchanted by witchcraft. No iron blade forged by human hands could pierce them.

"Leave him to me!" Beowulf cried. "We will all share the fruits of victory, but the battle is mine."

Grendel felt himself weakening. "Let me go," he snarled. "I have treasures beyond imagining hidden in the marsh. They are yours, if you release me."

"I care nothing for your treasures," said Beowulf, feeling his strength increase. He tightened his hold.

"If you let me go, I will leave Heorot Hall tonight and never return."

"You will never return because you will be dead," Beowulf replied. "Fight if you wish to live, cowardly monster. But only one of us will see the sun rise."

"Then I will fight!" roared Grendel. He and Beowulf wrestled the length of Heorot Hall, overturning benches, ripping down tapestries, splintering the gilded furniture that was Hrothgar's pride. Making one last effort to break that mighty grip, Grendel threw himself against Beowulf with all his strength.

Beowulf held firm. Grendel's shoulder burst. The monster shrieked as his whole arm came away from his body. He fled the hall, bellowing with pain and terror. Back to the marshes he ran, leaving a bloody trail across the fens. Death found him there. Grendel sank into the muck from which he came, never to rise again.

King Hrothgar and Queen Wealhtheow celebrated with a great feast. They rewarded Beowulf and his men with fine weapons, jewels, and other treasure. Hrothgar's warriors beat their swords against their shields to celebrate Beowulf's victory.

"The fight is fought; the deed is done. Let the story be told," said the king. And so it was.

> *From north to south on land or sea,*
> *Upon the earth or beneath the tall sky,*
> *Never lived a man equal to Beowulf,*
> *Ecgtheow's son, slayer of Grendel.*

Author's Note

Beowulf is the oldest surviving epic poem in English literature. However, the characters are not English. They are Vikings from what are now Sweden and Denmark, where the story takes place. The poem was written in Anglo-Saxon, the ancestor of modern English.

The full story of *Beowulf* consists of three parts. The first and best known is the hero's fight with Grendel. In the second part, Beowulf battles Grendel's mother, a sea witch, and becomes king of the Geats, the people of southern Sweden. In the third, Beowulf kills a dragon at the cost of his own life.

The story of *Beowulf* can be traced back to the sixth century. The poem itself was composed about two hundred years later. It survives in a single manuscript written during the tenth century, more than a thousand years ago. In 1731, a fire nearly destroyed the manuscript. A major work of English literature was almost lost forever. Since then scientists and scholars have worked to preserve what was left and recover what was damaged.

The original manuscript of *Beowulf* is one of the treasures of London's British Library. The latest translation of the poem, and one of the best, is *Beowulf: A New Verse Translation* by Seamus Heaney.

Also available today is *The Electronic Beowulf*, which uses the power of computers and digital imaging to increase our understanding of the poem. The project can be found on the Internet at *www.uky.edu/ArtsSciences/English/Beowulf/eBeowulf/guide.htm.*

For Mike and Gayle —E.A.K.

For Bill Reiss —L.E.F.

Copyright © 2005 by Shearwater Books
Illustrations copyright © 2005 by Leonard Everett Fisher
All rights reserved
Distributed in Canada by Douglas & McIntyre Publishing Group
Color separations by Chroma Graphics PTE Ltd.
Printed and bound in the United States of America by Berryville Graphics
Designed by Robbin Gourley and Jay Colvin
First edition, 2005
1 3 5 7 9 10 8 6 4 2

www.fsgkidsbooks.com

Library of Congress Cataloging-in-Publication Data
Kimmel, Eric A.
    The hero Beowulf / retold and adapted by Eric A. Kimmel from the epic poem Beowulf ;
pictures by Leonard Everett Fisher.— 1st ed.
        p. cm.
    Summary: A simple, brief retelling of the Anglo-Saxon epic about the heroic efforts of
Beowulf, son of Ecgtheow, to save the people of Heorot Hall from the terrible monster, Grendel.
    ISBN-13: 978-374-0-30671-7
    ISBN-10: 0-374-30671-0
    1. Beowulf—Adaptations—Juvenile literature. [1. Beowulf. 2. Folklore—England.]
I. Fisher, Leonard Everett, ill. II. Beowulf. III. Title.

PZ8.1.K567He 2005
[398.2]—dc22
[E]
                                                                                    2003054888